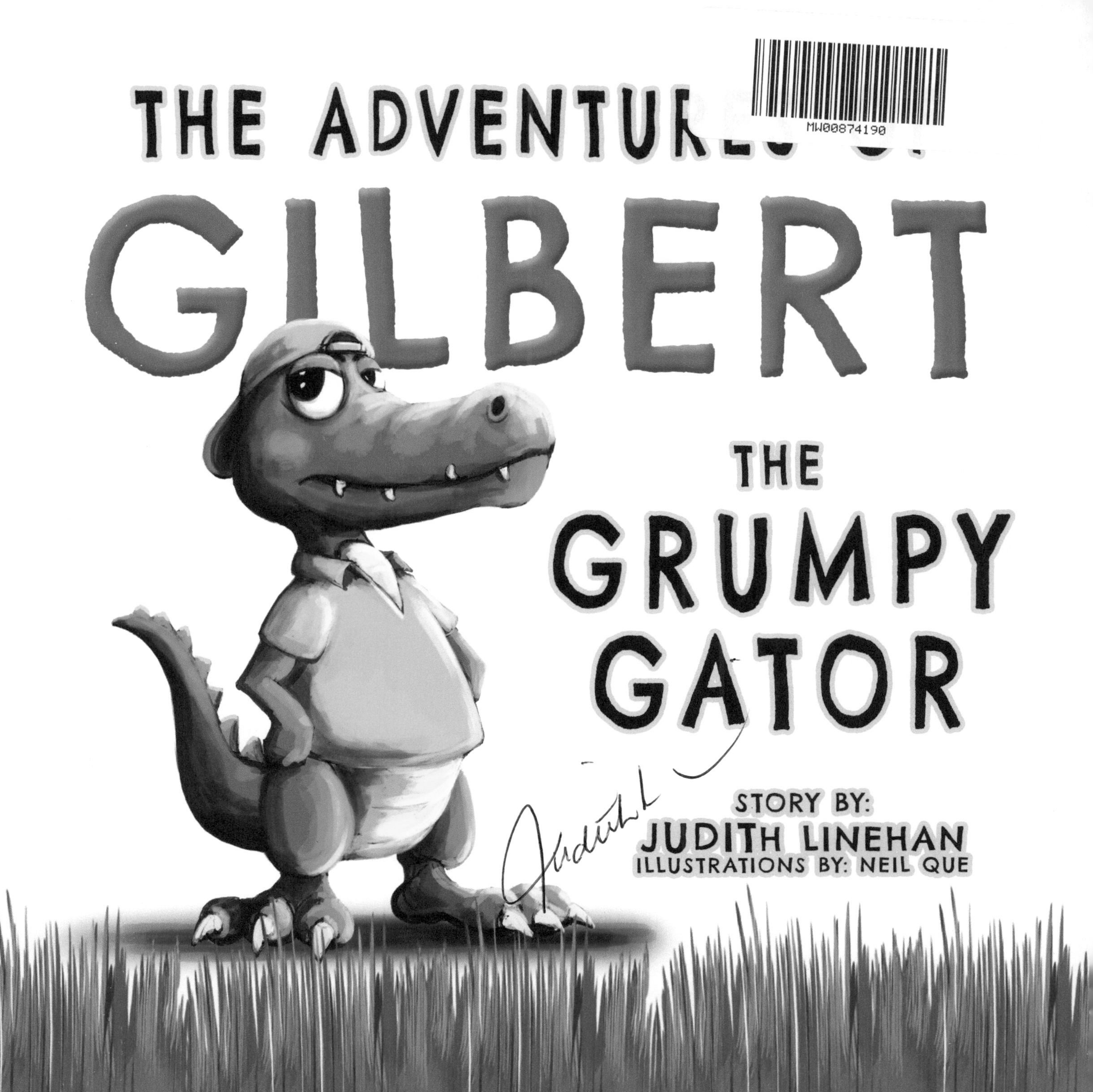
THE ADVENTURES OF
GILBERT
THE
GRUMPY
GATOR
STORY BY:
JUDITH LINEHAN
ILLUSTRATIONS BY: NEIL QUE

The Adventures of Gilbert the Grumpy Gator

ISBN 13: 978-1-7336855-0-4

Published in the United States
www.linehanauthors.com

Book design by Book Branders

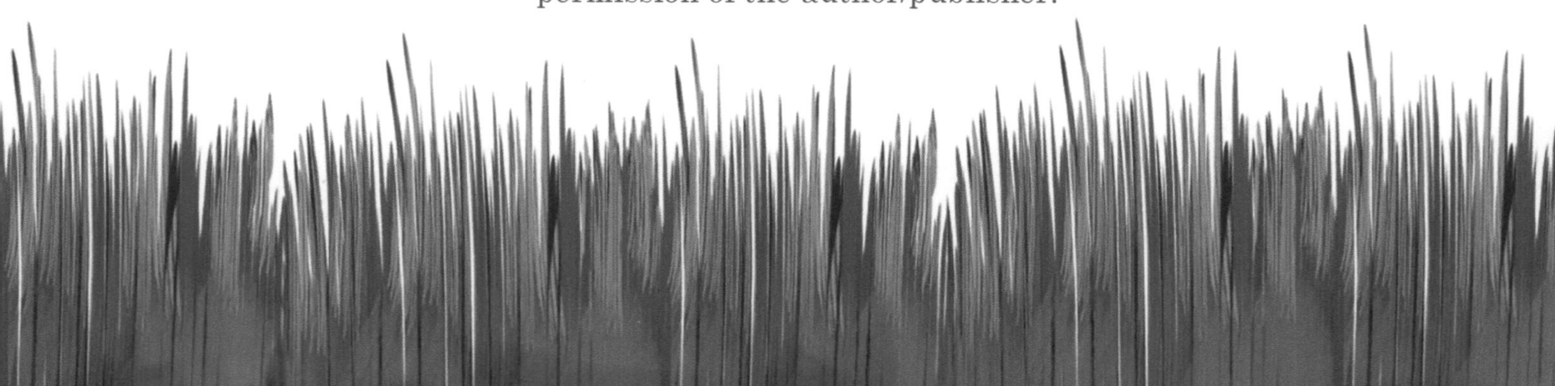

Dedication

To my father Henry Parker that
started me writing funny poems,
to my family for their encouragement
and especially my husband Thom (a
published author himself) for helping
me through the publishing process.
A special hug for my artistic son
Brett Hornung that brought
Gilbert to life!!

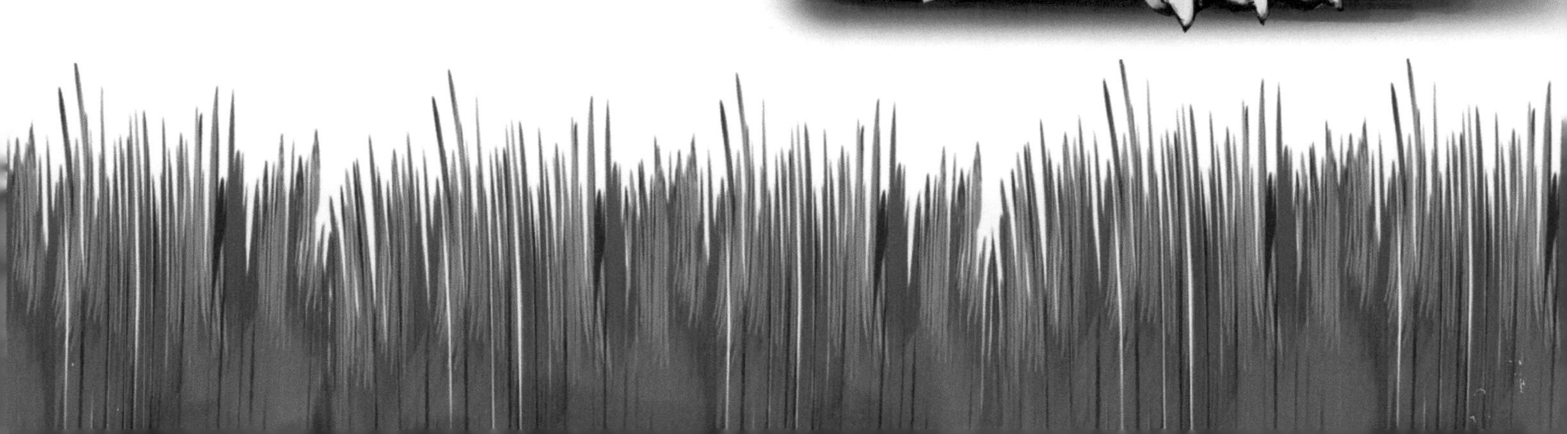

In a place not too far south
lived a gator named Gilbert
with a very large mouth.

His mother was Katie; his father was Brad. A little sister named Sammy that just made him mad.

He was always in trouble
with his mom and dad
for opening his mouth
and saying things bad.

So, early
one morning
while his parents
were sleeping,

Gilbert tiptoed
out; a new life
he was seeking.

He crept away
through a dreary
swamp not sure
where he was
heading and what
he may want.

At the end of
the swamp was
a very wide river.
When he entered
the current, his tail
was a quiver.

He crawled on the
bank to take a rest.
He was so weary,
so sleeping was best.
Z Z Z

When he woke up,
to his delight, he was
next to a diner that
said, "Open All Night."

Next to the diner
on more dry land
was a sign stating,
You're on The Grand
Strand!

Gilbert couldn't absorb
all he was seeing,
the noise and the cars
were a threat to his being.

He crawled towards a more grassy
site and saw some water, to his delight.

He decided he
needed to take
a swim, so he went
to the water and
finally dove in.

At the bottom of Lake Alex,
he could see nothing
but white.
It could be
dinner. What a
wonderful sight!

He opened his
mouth and
started to chew,
but something
stuck on his tooth.
It felt like a shoe.

Gilbert shook his tail and banged his head, but the object stayed there. It tasted like lead.

All of a sudden, his tooth really ached. He said, “What will I do, for goodness’ sake?”

He looked at his reflection to see what stuck to his jaw. A MoJo golf ball was what he saw.

He turned around and saw a sign. "Welcome to The Ledge: Golf That's Divine."

Another gator named Justin took a quick peek, "I know what to do and the place you must seek.

You need a human because they have hands to pull out the ball and toss in the sand.

Humans don't like us because we are scary, so we have to trick them not to be wary.
MOJO

So, we must go to a mini golf course and pretend to be a hole in one source."

The place we are going is on Chelsea Lane, across the street from Attorney Brendan Paine.

Off they went to Reptiles R Us.
A chip into the gator is a golf round must.

So, Gilbert and Justin, while it was dark, replaced the fake gator in the mini golf park.

Early the next morning, standing by the gate, were cousins Ashley and Andrew, hoping they weren't late.

They had free passes to Reptiles R Us but had to be there before the 10 o'clock bus.

They hoped their friends Chris, Olivia, and Maddy remembered their tickets bought by their daddy

They got there in time and picked up their gear and went to hole one and putt with no fear.

They played the hole with the frilled lizard and proceeded quickly to the terrapin wizard.

Alligator Alley was finally in sight,
so Andrew ran ahead just for spite.
At the last hole, their scores were even.

Without a clear winner,
they wouldn't be leaving.

Ashley hit first, hitting Gilbert's front claw. The ball bounced off his tail and into his jaw.

Andrew shot second, aiming for his mouth. His shot was wide and a little bit south.

So, Andrew hit again, falling behind.
He was losing the match, but he was resigned.

Ashley, the leader, picked up her ball.
Andrew got his, but that's not all.

As they were leaving,
"Hey, Ashley," he said.
"I may have lost, but
I found this MoJo instead."

Ashley asked Andrew, “Where was it found?”

He turned to show her, but the gator was gone.

So, Gilbert returned home
to his family center,

to tell mom, dad, and Sammy,
of his great adventure.

About the Author

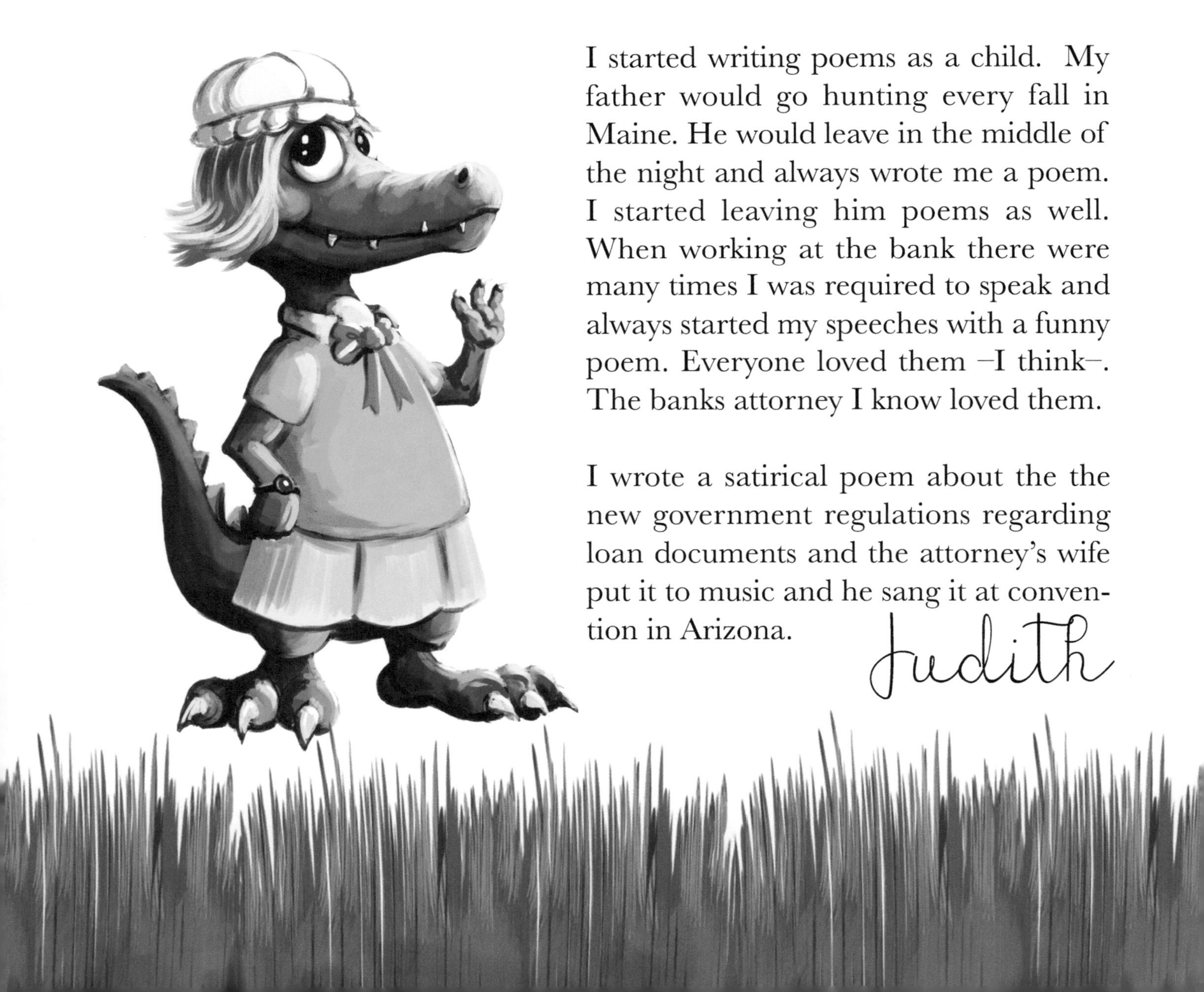

I started writing poems as a child. My father would go hunting every fall in Maine. He would leave in the middle of the night and always wrote me a poem. I started leaving him poems as well. When working at the bank there were many times I was required to speak and always started my speeches with a funny poem. Everyone loved them –I think–. The banks attorney I know loved them.

I wrote a satirical poem about the the new government regulations regarding loan documents and the attorney's wife put it to music and he sang it at convention in Arizona.

Judith

About Gilbert

My kids always like the children's books that rhymed the best. Dr. Seuss, Bill Peet and others so my son Brett suggested my poems were just as good and suggested I write my own books.

My husband and I play lots of golf here in South Carolina and one of my favorite courses is Oyster Bay in Sunset Beach, NC. We have seen up to 22 alligators in one day while playing. I have become fascinated with them so that's where the idea for Gilbert was born.

My son Brett Hornung drew Gilbert that the illustrator has based Gilbert's likeness to in the book. I also have fallen in love with the blue herons and wood storks and they are characters in other Gilbert books that will be published soon.

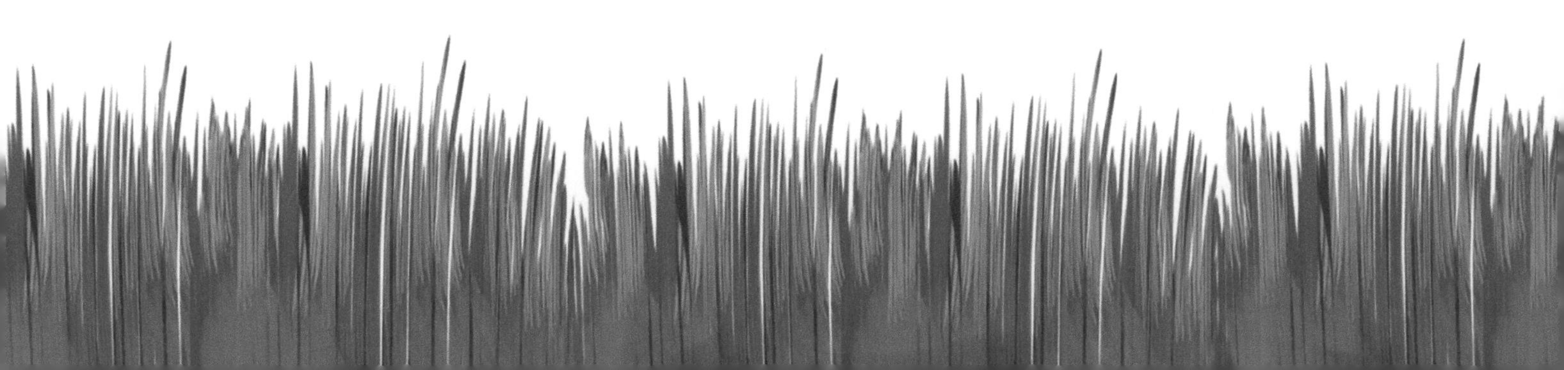

CPSIA information can be obtained
at www.ICGtesting.com
Printed in the USA
BVHW021134050419
544500BV00001B/1/P

* 9 7 8 1 7 3 3 6 8 5 5 0 4 *